The Ringers

RAVEN OAK

GREY SUN
PRESS
SEATTLE

The Ringers

For information address Grey Sun Press, PO Box 1635 Bothell, WA 98041

WWW.GREYSUNPRESS.COM

ISBN 978-1-947712-03-4

Library of Congress Control Number: *In Progress*

The Ringers

RAVEN OAK

GREY SUN PRESS

I t was an eerie fog if ever there was one.

If fog could envelop every pore of every creature, even then it could not be as dense and adhering as it was that night.

Far outside the grand city of Veleden cowered a village of silence. Whereas you or I might expect sugarplums and mirth in the early days of winter, the village of Dekwood embraced grays and blacks as evening fell, and its people secured their windows against the creeping fog.

Children buried themselves beneath well-worn quilts, but they didn't clamp their eyes shut. No, they slapped tiny hands over their ears to ward off the jingle-jangle of horses' reins as the Ringers approached.

A guardsman leaned across the jingle-jangle bridle of his perfectly normal-looking horse as it crossed the threshold into town. Snowflakes sprinkled across his red suit and blended in with his white sash. The four men in his brigade, if they could be called men, pulled up alongside him.

Five muzzles puffed frost into the air

Five men, skin haggard as it draped skeletal frames, sat astride the white beasts.

Five days they would ride and rid Dekwood of those unneeded, those too bold for purpose.

A lone child coughed as he huddled against a tree. Tears mingled with snot as he muffled his cries with a ragged scarf. The bells jangled, the eerie sound carrying through the eve like a death keen. The child froze like the snow beneath him, and five faces grinned.

One

TWO WEEKS UNTIL WINTER SOLSTICE

The day we sought refuge in Dekwood held no special purpose. Two seasons without work and my papa devised our bold plan. We would load up our belongings in a simple carriage and head north for better fortune.

I was fourteen, convinced I understood everything while understanding very little. It was a dark time to travel, but my mother's womb thickened with my brother and food grew scarce when the grand forests shriveled and died.

How does a forest die? Perhaps it was nothing more than a lack of rain or some magician's grim spell that shriveled the leaves mid-summer and rotted the bark 'til the logs fell without the help of a woodsman's axe. If logging was no longer lucrative, perhaps the more industrialized work of Dekwood could line my papa's pockets.

Five days' travel had left me without purpose. I taxed my mother's patience as I spoke of a spell to change rain into snow or the logic behind the life-giving elements that connected all living creatures and powered the magics of our world. When my feeble attempts to bring about snow froze my mother's morning tea, she hid my magical texts in a locked trunk. Their absence didn't stop me from walking beside the carriage to draw upon the soil's power. Every few hours' travel, I tugged the gloves from my fingers and spread them across the hard earth to feel the thrum of magic beneath me.

And when my mother wasn't watching, I'd whisper the words to call forth a slight dusting of snow across my brow. If she wondered why my red hair bore crystalline flecks, she remained as silent as our days on the road.

On the sixth day of travel, heavy snowflakes tickled my nose. They spread themselves across the hardened dirt road which snaked north to Veleden and south to the City of Escen. I'd never set foot in either, but I'd heard Tellers talk of the great magistrates who managed the towns of the North.

Rumors traveled about the Magistrate of Dekwood, an ageless and grim man who ruled from a hillside mansion. People said he mourned the loss of his sons. Whether from a factory accident or illness, I refrained from asking. Such tales were for *children*.

I was no mere child. I couldn't be if I wished to study magic. One day I would be a magician—capable of powerful magics to bring the trees to bloom and the rivers to flow.

And force the clouds to snow.

I opened my mouth to inquire after Dekwood, but my mother's pursed lips left me silent. My feet ached, but watching my mother struggle to maintain her posture on the bumpy trail made me glad to be walking alongside the carriage. Papa grinned down at me from the coachman's seat.

No manor homes or farms dotted the countryside nor any indication that we grew closer to our destination. I wrinkled my nose when a snowflake graced it, and my mother sighed. "Elise, if you continue to make such expressions, you'll gain wrinkles before you're wed."

Before my soon-to-be brother, an accident that puzzled

the Physics aplenty, my mother had spent her days raveling yarn at the seamstress's shop. Like a skein of yarn, wrinkles twined their way across her forehead, and I grinned. "Yours are what I love best about you."

My brashness earned me another scowl before she busied herself with her knitting.

I tried to follow the air across my mother's belly to hear the whispers of my brother—as the Physics had done when my mother had taken ill—but it was only wind to me, the magic far beyond my abilities.

"Papa," I said, and his wood-warped hands tightened on the reins. "Will Dekwood have a school? Something beyond the elementary standard? Perhaps someone with magical knowledge to prepare me for the entrance exams?"

Firm fingers loosened their grip. "Any place that close to the City of Veleden is bound to have something. You'll be back to your preparations in no time."

Day ten brought us over yet another hill. A gritty forest loomed ahead like something out of a nightmare, and I shivered beneath my woolen cloak. "Are we to travel through there?" I asked.

His skin paled as we observed the swaying tree-corpses that cast long shadows across the trail. "Don't tell your mother. Go distract her while we pass."

I peeked in the carriage's window. My mother lay across the crunchy, thin-padded seat, eyes closed and breath slow. Her pale hair was messed against a pillow. "She's sleeping." I glanced at the trees and whispered, "But let's hurry."

The whites of his eyes reflected his fear, an odd emotion in a man who scaled great heights for his trade, and I shivered.

"Agreed. Last we need is your mother carrying on about evil curses cast upon our future." My papa laid a superstitious hand upon his heart.

Winter tightened its grip on the dead oak, and their bones

shivered. Even barren, the trees' branches stretched across the sky and blotted out all light. Like the shriveled fingers of the dead they drooped down and reached for us, stealing our warmth and joy before we were more than a foot into the woods.

Nothing lived in these trees.

No sound besides the muffled hoof beats in frozen snow. No smell beyond the burn of cold air in the nostrils. Branches snagged along my cloak, and I pulled it tighter across my shoulders.

I held my breath 'til I thought I might burst. When I glanced at the spot beside me, my papa did the same and I laughed. The glee bounced beyond us and reverberated back, amplified and shrill.

"Hush," he whispered.

Every now and again, the marks of a woodsmith scored the narrow tree trunks, and a hollow log lay beside our path, a fallen soldier in the battle of survival. And so we traveled for nigh two candlemarks.

Just as we broke free of the forest, my mother sneezed and startled a shrill cry from my lips. "Control yourself, Elise," she said through the carriage's open front window. "A young lady need not give in to such whimsies."

She met my gaze but her death grip on her shawl relayed how long she had been awake.

Papa tapped my shoulder.

Nestled among the countryside's hills, homes rose from the hard earth, their rooftops covered in winter and chimneys smoking with warmth. A great warehouse marred the image, as did the grim mansion on a hill. Dekwood.

Papa grinned. "Welcome home."

Two

THREE DAYS UNTIL THE SOLSTICE

No one greeted us. No children scattered snow in the streets or chased a dog into alley carts. A few faces peered out dirty windows the size of dinner plates before fading into darkness.

At the village's center stood a grotesque statue of a man too tall, with a grin too wide that stretched his mouth past redemption. His horse-like teeth were carved of marble, and his hands held a skein of wool.

"Who's that?" I asked.

"The magistrate maybe?" guessed Papa. "Can't think who else would get a statue made of polished stone."

My mother tapped on the glass. "We've a place to go tonight, don't we?"

"From the magistrate. Said so in his letter."

The horses slowed before a brick monstrosity two stories high with edges of cast iron beams and cobbled bricks and stone. Not a brick out of place, and yet the dingy gray embraced the building and marred its appearance.

My mother alighted from the carriage with Papa's assistance. "What is this place?"

"Welcome to the inn," Papa said. He tied the reins to the post out front with a clove hitch.

"Surely we're not staying *here*, are we? Where will the horses be stabled? And the carriage?" My mother pouted at the imposing building, not at all to her customary taste. Inside, loosely grouped chairs and tables gathered dust. A single patron sat at the bar, completely ignoring us.

The woman behind the counter gave Papa a light smile. "You must be Erol Jankin. We've been wonderin' when you'd get here." She squeezed wide hips through the bar opening and ambled over to us, thick pink skirt ruffles dusting the floor as she moved. "The name's Beatrice."

My mother ignored the woman's offered hand, but Papa seized it with exaggerated enthusiasm. "Thanks for the welcome. Noticed quite an oddity on the trip here—that...forest "

Beatrice gave him a curt nod. "You're welcome to two rooms upstairs 'til you can get somethin' of your own. The carriage and horses outside?"

Papa nodded. "In his letter, the magistrate said he'd board the horses—sell the carriage to cover room and board."

"For you and the missus, maybe, but the rooms're too small for the three of you. You'll need another room."

My mother's mouth popped open. "We'd be indebted to this magistrate."

Beatrice's soot-colored eyes settled on the heap of books in my arms. The woman paled at the infinity symbol on the cover, and said, "Shouldn't be long before something comes available, I wager."

The lone patron excused himself as my mother voiced her complaints. Papa forced a smile as Beatrice handed him two keys. "Ain't a kitchen or anything in the rooms, but there's a restaurant 'cross the way that serves meals. I've got the usual helpin's of meat and potatoes in the evenin'. Bread and cheese in the mornin'. I lock up at midnight. If you aren't inside by then, you'll be locked out."

Papa pocketed both keys, ignoring my outstretched hand. "Thank you."

"Won't I need my key?" I asked, and my mother shushed me. "Mother, I'm fourteen. If I am old enough to attend the Academe, surely I could be trusted with my key?"

"No, ma'am." Beatrice wagged a plump finger at me. "You listen to your folks. Stay in your rooms at night, no matter what you...hear."

"What would we hear?" I asked.

"Bells."

My mother tugged me toward the stairs.

"Bells?" I asked.

"I'll send Vincent to help you unload your belongin's," said Beatrice, and Papa nodded his thanks.

Three steps from the top, I turned to face my mother. "The bells of the spirits? Is that what she meant?"

My mother pressed a finger to my lips. "Don't make trouble."

When I opened my mouth, Papa shook his head. "Listen to your mother."

I didn't know what shocked me more—that there were spirits in town or that Papa agreed with my mother. Either way, I was determined to remain awake and listen for the bells.

Three

TWO DAYS UNTIL THE SOLSTICE

Morning brought a misty rain to Dekwood. We stood in the town square, woolen jackets doing little to keep the chill off our shoulders. Either the bells had never sounded, or I'd fallen asleep.

A little slip of a man rushed over to us. Raindrops dripped off his umbrella and splashed upon my plaits.

"Are you Erol Jankin?" he asked, and Papa nodded. "I'm Magistrate du Leunt's assistant. The magistrate sends his most profound apologies."

"Erol, you said—"

Papa patted my mother's gloved hands, tightly knotted over her thickened waist. "I understand, Mr...?"

"Nicolas Ashton. The magistrate can hardly meet everyone who stumbles into town, no matter how...desperate their letters may appear. I'm sure you understand, Mrs. Jankin." He tipped his hat in my mother's direction.

To my father, he said, "I understand your former occupation was a logger in Devlon. I'm afraid we don't have a need for such work. If you wish to pay back your debt to the magistrate—"

"I was given to believe our carriage would cover our time at the inn," said my mother.

"Your carriage was hardly fit to cover your stay for a day, let alone a lengthier time." My mother glared at Papa.

Whatever the magistrate had arranged, our plans had changed. My mother squared her shoulders before she spoke. "Then I'm afraid we must take our leave of Dekwood."

Papa whispered something in her ear. Her face paled before her cheeks flushed like a ripe strawberry.

"As I was saying, men work in the leather mill or out in the fields with the sheep." Mr. Ashton frowned as he noted Papa's lanky figure. "I suppose you'll do with the tanner. Little old for apprenticing but work hard, and you could clear your sizeable debt in perhaps a year's time."

Sizeable? We had slumbered here one evening yet our debt was sizeable? Tuition for the Academe would stretch us beyond our means with my mother's need for society life, but surely a few seasons missed work had not brought us to such dire straits? Papa's hand rested on my shoulder, and I bit my tongue.

"Women and those not able-bodied work in the textile factory. Everyone pulls their share in Dekwood," continued Mr. Ashton.

"I'll admit to never having worked with leather before, but I figure can't be much harder than climbing trees in the nippy winter. Say, I was going to ask the magistrate about schools."

"School?"

"Yes, for Elise. Back in Devlon, she was readying for entrance into the—"

The man's nose twitched with impatience as he waved a hand at Papa. "She's too old for school here. As long as she's got the basics, she has all she needs. Doesn't take much by way of brains to work in the factory, now does it?"

"The factory? But sir, I'm to study magic at the—"

Like a striped tomcat of Devlon, the man hissed as he stepped back. "Magic isn't tolerated or needed in Dekwood. You'll be working in the factory or none at all."

"Then I'll take none, sir, as I have studies to attend to." Papa's fingers pinched my shoulder, and I winced.

"If you know what's good for you, you'll nip that in the bloom now," Mr. Ashton said to Papa with the wag of his finger. "If you want to stay in Dekwood, these are your options." Papa nodded and Mr. Ashton continued. "Work begins an hour after sunrise. Report to the tanner's at noon, and he'll fill you in on the rest. It's just down the street a few buildings and on the right."

"What about housing?"

His eyes, thin charcoal slits at the bottom of too large a forehead, rested on me, and that grin returned. "You shouldn't be too long in the inn."

He'd made it three steps toward the mansion in the distance when Papa called out, "We'll be in contact if we need something. Thank you, and thank the magistrate."

My mother elbowed him in the ribs. "When were you going to tell me of our debt? Had I realized we'd amassed so much in Devlon—" Her cheeks flushed as she turned her eyes on me. Unusually frizzy hair popped out from beneath her wide-brimmed hat, whose red poinsettias clashed with the rich plum of her scarf. She tucked the escapee behind her ear. "Dally about in the rain if you wish, but I've no purpose in this...mess."

We trailed behind her to the inn. A wide road such as this should have played host to many, yet it remained empty. My mother tugged on the doorknob of the inn's solitary door, but the swollen wood stuck.

Papa gave it a good tug and when it released its grip, my mother had an additional reason to scowl so early in the day.

The door banged shut behind her. "She'll find reason enough to smile once our situation's settled," said Papa.

I only half heard him as I studied the rain. Like the town, winter here lacked its usual patterns.

As if he'd followed my thoughts, Papa said, "I suspect everyone's at the leather mill or the textile factory. Odd little town this is."

"Am I to join everyone in the factory?"

He sighed. "You've heard more than you should, but your papa's gone and gotten himself into...a delicate situation. It's just 'til we can afford to send you to the Academe."

I frowned.

Something about this town didn't feel temporary—the way people's drooping shoulders matched their mouths, the way buildings held a hint of desperation with their creaks and wobbles. This town didn't release folks to bigger and better things. It kept them tight within its clutches.

Forever.

A shiver pricked goose pimples along my arms, and something deep within the earth made my nose itch.

"What is it?" Papa asked, and I shook my head.

There was no reason to be suspicious of someone using magic, but after Mr. Ashton's reaction to the word, I tucked away the reminder to investigate further. Something just wasn't right in this town.

ONE DAY UNTIL THE SOLSTICE

My disappointment with the lack of bells warred with curiosity the next morning. The factory doors towered far above my red head. Moss grew between the doorframe bricks, and rust stained the mortar. When I stepped through the doorway and didn't feel magic's touch at my feet, I sighed. A shove from behind sent me sprawling face-first along the floor's dead planks.

"You're blocking the door. Get a move on." The gruff voice's owner shuffled past me, leaving me a spectacular view of worn boot-heels and a coarse gray cloak. My mother's frizzy hair blocked my view of the factory as she knelt, her hand thrust out to take mine. If my mother had been a magic user, the owner of the worn boots would have needed a new pair. Instead, she helped me to my feet and glared as others passed.

From the disabled who hobbled in with canes clutched in knobbed fingers, to the mother with a baby strapped to her hip, women and children of all ages and sizes filed into the factory.

Large looms stretched nigh the full length of the floor, crammed against each other. Wedged in each corner rose four staircases. Women settled into their weaving with a simple rhythm while the children lined up against the front wall.

"You must be the new ones," said a man with a scruffy beard tucked into the collar of his shirt. My gaze landed on the top of his balding head, and I hid my grin. "You—" He jabbed his finger at me. "Join the other children."

My mother inclined her head, and I trudged over to stand behind a girl shaking rain out of her cloak. The man with the long beard led my mother toward the building's rear, and I shivered in the damp chill. "Who was that?" I asked the girl before me.

"That's the Tackler."

"The what?"

She tilted her head toward the looms. "Looms are in-intra-inter—"

"Intricate?"

"Intricate machines. When they aren't behaving, the Tackler fixes them to work so them on the looms can weave. You're the new one, aren't you?"

A girl older than my fourteen years shushed us as the Tackler approached.

"Good—you've already met Charlene," he said.

The blonde folded her cloak and set it on the floor without response.

I pulled mine tighter about my shoulders. "Yes, sir—" His thin nostrils flared, and I ceased speaking and joined the others in a rigid line that snaked around the interior walls.

We followed him silently—not that it would have mattered much with the looms' racket. The queue stopped beside a woman who pumped a foot treadle as her deft hands spun wool through the loom's grid. The Tackler gestured to a girl at the front of the line. "You turned sixteen yesterday, correct?" The girl who had silenced me earlier nodded. "You'll be working with Rebecca to learn the loom until you've developed the skill to weave on your own."

The girl's cheeks flushed at what obviously was intended to be praise, and I bit my tongue. Nothing about this job piqued my interest. A hundred or so women sat on hard stools in silence as they worked with hand and foot in a loud, drafty room. My mind itched for my books, but I followed along wordlessly as the line resumed its movement toward the rear of the building. The Tackler opened two doors and ushered us into a room the size of our old home in Devlon.

I followed Charlene to two stools against the wall. "I'm Elise."

She nodded and pulled two stiff-bristled brushes from a nearby basket. Charlene handed them to me and asked, "Ever carded wool before?"

"Never in my life."

She raised a brow and shoved a small basket of wool into my lap. Her demonstration with the carders proved thorough, but when I tried my hand at it, the wool caught in the spines of the brush. "You're pulling too hard. Be gentle," she said. She stretched the wool until it formed a uniform swath moving in a single direction. Thirty strokes later, mine remained a mass of fibers moving at odds with each other.

"It takes practice?" I asked. While Charlene shrugged, several children hid laughs behind oily hands.

"My ma says your ma used to sew for fancy ladies in Devlon. Is that true?" asked Charlene, and I nodded. "Then how'd you end up so...unskilled?"

I smiled. "My gran says I was destined for greater things."

It had been a point of contention between my mother and my paternal grandmother—right up until she had passed the year before. My gran had studied magic until she had married at her parent's insistence. It was her wrinkled fingers that had first touched mine to the soil and taught me of power.

The gentle lull of brushing the wool relaxed my shoulders, and my head dipped toward my chest until Charlene kicked my ankle. I jerked my head upright to find a woman old enough to be my grandmother in the doorway. I squirmed beneath her gaze until a few giggles caught her attention. "Remove your cloak," she barked.

"I'll catch a chill. Please, I'm not used to...such conditions."

More giggles, which she silenced with a look. Despite her bony frame, strong fingers tugged at my cloak and forced me to my feet. Both carders clattered against the wood floor. I towered over her and with the hunch in her back, she struggled to look me in the face. I straightened my cloak.

The others stared at their wool with rapt fascination. "You're new, so I'll forgive your insolence today. But tomorrow, I expect better. You aren't well-to-do no more, so don't be expecting no favors. Tomorrow, you'll leave your cloak with the rest."

When the doors closed, Charlene released the breath she'd been holding. "Is that woman normally so cross?" I asked, but she rotated her stool until her back was to me.

To keep myself awake, I sketched incantations in my head and wordlessly recited formulas until my hands were stiff and my stomach threatened to pierce my backbone with hunger. When two o'clock arrived, the other children pulled lunches from their satchels. Their meal was punctuated by brief whispers. My feet were nearly numb after half a day on a wooden stool, and I bent over to touch my hands to the floor before rolling up to a standing position. My hand was on the chilly doorknob when someone touched my shoulder.

"Where're you going?"

A boy stood behind me, a roll of bread between his fingers. "To find my mother," I said.

"Can't." His hand against the door kept it firmly shut.

"But my mother has my meal."

"She'll be working now. Her lunch brief was at one," he said.

"I promise I won't bother her. I just wish to fetch my lunch from her bag."

An old puffy scar beneath his eye twitched. "You'll have to eat later. Can't interrupt the weavers."

"But—"

He pried my fingers from the doorknob and once free, pressed one of them against the puffy scar beneath his right eye. "If you interrupt the work, we all suffer, see?"

I jerked my finger away and returned to my stool, though my stomach grumbled audibly. Charlene handed me a wedge of cheese and some dried apple bits.

"Thank you," I said.

"No, thank you."

I got the feeling she was thanking me for remaining in the room, and I asked, "Is it like this every day?"

"Like what?" she whispered.

"Silent. Dejected."

The boy with the scar pressed his lips together, but otherwise ignored us. "There's too much to do for idle chat," she mumbled as she nibbled on a hunk of bread.

"I've never worked before, but surely you could talk while carding—at least as good as you are."

Someone shuffled by the closed doors. Once the person passed, Charlene asked, "You've never worked?"

"No."

"Then whatcha do before?"

"I went to school."

Scar boy laughed. "We've all been to school. What did you do after that?"

"I'm not referring to the elementary standard. I was studying for entrance into the Academe." When Charlene cocked her head, I added, "The Arcane Academe of Veleden."

Two dozen children edged their stools away from me. Those still seated on the ground drew their feet under themselves. "Don't tell anyone," said Charlene. "Magic isn't allowed here."

"Why?"

The boy with the scar strode over and stopped an inch from my face. Mutton and the hint of apple soured my nose. "If you want to survive, stop drawing attention to yourself. Stop asking questions."

"But questions are how one learns—"

"Not in Dekwood."

This time, when the shuffle returned to the door, it didn't pass. The old woman stepped inside, a brown satchel in her hands. "Your mother made quite the fuss 'bout you gettin' this." She thrust the patchwork bag in my direction.

No one in the room glanced at the old woman, but they were aware of her every movement. Even the seven-year-old in the corner watched from the corner of her eyes. I took my meal, but I was no longer hungry. How could I survive this town? How could my parents?

Charlene would accept none of my lunch, not that there was any time. We returned to our labors after little more than three bites. The older children shifted from carding to spinning the wool into long threads on spindles. By the time work ended, my arms and back ached. No one complained, nor did they limp or tremble as I did.

My mother's pale head bobbed in the mass outside the room but quickly disappeared as bodies shuffled toward the drafty building's exit. My shoulders brushed against silent townies, and I'd nearly reached the front door when something tugged on my cloak. I had neared the doorframe when I felt another tug.

"Elise," someone whispered, and rough hands propelled me through the door. The bright sun made my eyes water until Charlene's gray form blocked the setting sun. "Elise, I needed to warn you to be careful."

"What reason would I need to be cautious?"

Charlene bit the edge of her lip. "Stop asking questions."

Before I could pry further, she vanished into the throng of workers. Someone tapped me upon the shoulder—my mother. Her shoulders drooped like decayed flesh. "I used to enjoy weaving." She rubbed her expanding middle and frowned. "I hope your father doesn't mind another round of the restaurant's corned beef."

Dinner bearing the consistency of an eraser didn't rest easy with my mind or my stomach, but my muscles screamed for sustenance and rest. It would have to suffice.

Like toy soldiers we formed a line that marched from the factory into the center of town, and from there, bodies separated to their homes without chatter or smiles. As my mother and I trudged toward the inn that served as our temporary home, snowflakes began to fall.

Five

THE SOLSTICE

Papa might have possessed the patience for corned beef, but little else that evening had given him pleasure. My questions about the oddness of such a town had fallen by the wayside, as had my complaints about working in the factory rather than preparing for the Academe. His words were placations for ears too young to comprehend their warning.

My ability to attend the bells that evening had waned as exhaustion had set in. My eyes had closed the moment I had tucked myself beneath the scratchy woolen blanket.

When sleep released me the next morning, the inn retained its usual silence and my parents' room lay empty. On the table rested a scribbled note bearing Papa's scrawl.

If you felt like I did yesterday, I figured you deserved the day off. Use it for study, eh? Your mother will tell the factory you've caught a chill. I'll be at work if you need something. There is some bread and cheese in the breadbox.

The cheese was a touch too sharp and the bread just this

side of stale, but they numbed my hunger. Outside, snow coated the cobblestone road and dotted the rooftops white against the gray sky. Tempted as I was to stroll past the factory and stick my tongue out at its closed door, the opportunity for a "holiday" pushed sense into my head. Besides, the crudeness of such a gesture would have set my mother to vapors.

The streets were as devoid of children and merchants as the day we had arrived. The town held its breath as its people worked—though for what purpose, I couldn't see. I tucked myself between two buildings and pressed my hand to the cobble, but the crumbling stone blocked any tingle of magic.

The door to the factory protested as it opened and closed, and I tried to sink into the cobble behind me. Charlene frowned at me from the alleyway's end, and I relaxed.

She said, "I thought you were sick."

"I caught a chill but upon waking, felt the air calling to me. Perhaps it might lend health to my lungs."

"Is that magic talk?" she asked, and I inclined my head. "See, that's the very thing that won't sit well with the magistrate."

"What would I care if the magistrate takes pleasure in my speech?"

She leaned against the building and closed her eyes. For all her youth, her frustration aged her and the eyes she turned on me could have been my mother's. "Take care, Elise. People who don't know their place tend to disappear."

"Disappear how?"

"I shouldn't say, but...it's only fair that you know, being new. Have you heard the bells?"

I shivered. "I tried to listen for them our first evening here, but they never came."

Charlene's eyes widened. "Be glad they never came, Elise. Be glad! What do you know of them?"

"Nothing much. Everyone in Dekwood fears them, which

makes little sense. Christmas approaches. We should be ringing the bells to welcome the coming of a new year and the gifts of our health and fortunes. To remember the dead and celebrate the future." Her eyes darted to the road as if she expected something, and I tilted my head. "Charlene, why do you dally with me? Shouldn't you be at the factory?"

"I was sent by the Tackler to search for you."

"For what purpose?"

She glanced a third time at the snow-covered street. "To make sure you were being truthful when it was said you'd taken ill." My snickering carried, and Charlene reached up to clap a hand over my mouth. "Shhh, they'll hear you."

"Who? The factory workers? Drafty though the walls may be, they would hear naught over the loom's thrum."

"No, not the workers. The Ringers."

"Beatrice, the innkeeper spoke of something unnatural in the bells. I've heard talk of spells that can commune with our ancestors, but never with foul intentions. Are these Ringers spirits then?"

"They aren't living. I don't know what they are."

The alleyway dimmed, and I flattened myself against the wall with Charlene. Our movements hid little as the inn keeper glared at us. "I knew you were up to no good. And Charlene—" She jabbed a finger at the girl, whose bottom lip trembled. "—what would your father say to hear you've been talkin' about things better left unsaid? Do you wish to court trouble this close to Christmas?"

The girl squeezed past the innkeeper. I placed a gloved hand on my hip—a gesture my mother would have abhorred—and nodded in the direction Charlene had darted. "I do not see what business it is of yours what Charlene and I discuss."

"Charlene should be at work in the factory, as should you." The innkeeper stopped my sideways motion with a firm grip on my elbow. "Your family's new here, so you don't understand our town and our ways. But the Ringers aren't nothin' to laugh at, and if you know what's good for you, you'll leave it well enough alone."

She didn't stop me as I brushed by, but my insides quaked. I expected a child to fear the boogieman looming in the shadows, but for an adult to fear one so, lent credence to the idea that it was more than a mere spirit or specter—possibly something magical in origin.

Possibly something more dangerous than I was prepared for.

I could have returned to the factory like the young woman my mother wished I was, but I could not. Magical study drew rule breakers and thinkers—people who wished to make order of magic's chaotic nature. If I were to understand these Ringers, I needed information.

And for that, I was going to need my books.

MY LIBRARY RESTED SOUNDLY inside the worn leather chest in my room. The dull buckle remained latched, though the chest had been pushed away from the door. A basin held fresh water from the innkeeper's visit to my room, which was perhaps when she had discovered my escape.

Papa's employ had provided us a certain level of influence in our previous home of Devlon, though not as much as my mother had wished. Despite our more affluent standing, we were held in little regard by those with true wealth. We had ignored my mother's ostentatious nature while saving up for my first year texts at the Academe. My fingers remained gloved as I removed both books from the chest.

The *Livre de Cantus* held the basic foundation for magical studies, and I set it aside. *The Histoires de Créabet Magia,* though, bore the history of magics and creatures of the known world.

I was convinced the answer lay within its pages, but several hours passed, leaving me with nothing more than a stiff neck and aching shoulders. A two-sentence paragraph on the probable existence of ghosts was the only reference to the undead in the entire tome. Nothing on bells or creatures with bells that caused people to disappear.

Information on the undead required a library— specifically, a library with the books of the grand arcanum. A town this small wouldn't have one...or would it? The first day we had arrived, I had felt the thrum of magic.

Downstairs, the innkeeper's fingers were lost to a pile of yarn and knitting needles. She ignored me until I stood beside her, then she glanced up from her needles with a cocked brow. "Do you need somethin'?" she asked, needles still clicking.

"Does this town have a library?"

The yarn wrapped around her index finger stilled. "Do you need a book to keep you company during your...illness?" I nodded, and she fetched a hardbound book from beneath the bar. "This here's a new mystery. Just finished it last week."

"I was hoping to choose my own reading material—" Her scowl deepened, and I retrieved the book from her waiting hand. "Thank you. But if I finish this and wish to read more, is there a library in town?"

"Not enough folks in town read for a library to be necessary. Ol' Henry does us right enough."

"Ol' Henry?" I asked.

"Local trader. Comes by once a month with whatever he picks up out in the world. A few books, some fabrics and yarns, random bits and things. You make sure that book takes no harm. Cost me a scarf and a good bottle of wine."

If someone possessed the books I needed, they weren't sharing. But then, most of the town kept tight lipped. The needles resumed their clicking as I left the inn. Only one person had opened up to me, and she was at the factory.

THE FACTORY'S front door loomed like the coming snow, and as I crept through, I waited for the Tackler to pounce. His shiny head never made an appearance, though one elder worker nearby thwacked her knuckles on a loom's wooden frame as she worked. No one glanced up, but they shivered in the cold wind that accompanied me through the entryway. The looms' humming drowned out the closing door's snap and those of my footsteps as I sought the rear carding room.

One left turn too many had me lost.

In front of me stood a woman whose wrinkles carried wrinkles. Rather than throwing a wooden shuttle through the floor to ceiling loom, the woman used a metal rod to weave bright colored wool by hand. She hunched over her weaving, her nose nearly touching the wool, and added tiny starburst patterns to a bright blue sky.

"I'm sorry to interrupt, but..." If she heard me, she made no indication, and I stepped closer to the loom. "I said I'm sorry—"

The old woman set the rod aside and cocked her head. I tried again. "I'm Elise, and I appear to be lost." Her mouth moved with slow, exaggerated movements but without sound. "I don't understand—"

"You'll get nothing out of her," said a rough voice. The boy with the scar stood behind me, a basket full of washed wool in his hands. "So many years in the factory, everyone goes deaf."

"She tried to say something. Or at least I thought she did," I said and followed when he gestured for me to do so.

"She was just mee-mawing at you. You'll need to work

here a span longer than a day to understand all that nonsense. Besides, I thought you were sick."

My cheeks grew warm despite the chill of the building. "The illness passed, so I decided to return to work."

His basket full of wool bounced, and he pursed already-too-thin lips together. His expression read, *you'd-have-to-be-insane-to-come-back*, but I shrugged it off.

"I became lost and decided to ask directions. What is mee-mawing?"

"The loomers talk without sound, through lip-reading and miming, though I suspect sometimes they just make it up." We turned right where I had turned left and ten feet later, we stood before the double doors to the carding room.

Charlene dropped her carder when I entered, and one of the older girls behind her said, "I thought you said she's sick."

I ignored the jibe and took my place beside Charlene. While yesterday had proven a quiet affair, the youngest children chattered in the corner while those older and nearing apprenticeship gossiped in whispers. I leaned closer to Charlene. "Is it true there is no library in Dekwood?"

"I think there's one in Magistrate Leunt's mansion. My dad mentioned it once. Why?"

"My books lacked the details on a particular research, but if I could perhaps look it up, that may give me answers. How do you function without a library or proper schooling?"

Charlene glanced up from her wool, but no one paid any attention to us in the hum of conversation. "Magistrate Leunt says there's no need for school beyond the basics. What use would we have for such knowledge working here?"

"But haven't you ever wondered why the sky is blue? Or why the snow only falls in the winter?"

Charlene shrugged, but her eyes lit up like buds on spring trees.

I asked, "Or why the trees outside this town have died?"

Several voices paused, awaiting Charlene's answer. "I…" She glared at the boy with the scar—who shared the same pointed chin and green eyes. Only a sibling could level such a look that flushed her skin, but Charlene was daring and she answered me in a quaverless voice. "I asked my dad once why other towns live with joy and food and warmth while ours shrivels like the forest outside. He wouldn't answer."

Air whistled between clenched teeth, and the boy with the scar crossed the room with a dozen steps. He leaned over and whispered something in Charlene's ear.

"No, Matthew, I won't be quiet," said Charlene. "Elise's right. Why don't we have a school anymore? Why is magic forbidden if it's a gift from the gods?"

She rattled off a litany of questions, but my brain latched onto one in particular. *Magic forbidden? It really was forbidden here?* I'd never encountered such a rule or law, but the idea made sense when added to people's reactions. Lost in thought, I missed the door opening and the hush that draped across the room. Something rough slapped my motionless hand, and I tumbled back into the real world.

"—Asleep again? Why aren't you working?" The woman before me lacked an arm, yet her single hand was rough, her fingers bearing the same calluses of the other weavers.

She raised her hand to slap mine again, and I shook my head. "My apologies," I muttered as I dragged the carder across the wool in my other hand. The woman nodded, but her narrowed eyes followed me as she paced. For ten minutes the room held its breath and worked, and only when the disfigured woman departed did the group return to a hesitant chatter.

Charlene's breath tickled my ear as she leaned close. "My father has a few books. I…I might be able to get them for you."

"Thanks, but I'm looking for something in particular."

"I know, that's what I mean. I've seen them—they have special covers and—"

I clapped my hands over hers to still them. "Wait, your father owns books on magic? Why would your father have those?"

"You met him the other day at the statue. He works for Magistrate Leunt."

Matthew cast aside his work and returned to Charlene's side. He hauled her up by bony wrists and dragged her into the corner where the youngest children worked. "You'll sit here until you can learn your place," he said and glared at me as he fetched her carders.

My fingers tingled in the cold room. The wooden floor kept me from the earth's soil, but moisture licked the air and brushed my cheek with the echo of magic. Air was trickier—thinner and more temperamental—but I set aside the carders and splayed my fingers across the surface of the air.

At first, my fingers remained chilled as I whispered the word for warmth, but after a few minutes, my fingertips flashed with sudden warmth. Sweat broke out across my forehead and trickled down my chin.

The air rose a degree at most before the energy fizzled. I slumped over, my breath haggard. Children stared and whispered. Across the room, Charlene's mouth hung open.

"Get back to work," snapped Matthew.

He did not look in my direction, but the edges of his shoulders and chin left me trembling. Rather than thanks for a warmer room, the children left me in frigid silence. At day's end, Matthew whisked his sister away before I could inquire further about the books. My mother frowned to see me, but must have noted the tension in my shoulders as we left. The walk home remained as silent as my afternoon had been.

I pled out of another corned beef dinner, instead choosing to curl up with the book the innkeeper had loaned me. My eyelids drooped as I turned the pages of yet another boring text that lacked the magic and adventure of the real world. The light peal of jingling bells reached my ears as the book fell against my nose, but when I opened my eyes, the sound was gone. Morning had come.

Six

THREE DAYS UNTIL CHRISTMAS

I'd grown accustomed to the hum of the looms and the hiss of their whispers. When they vanished, my ears grew acutely aware of the bitter silence in the factory. Before, villagers had offered brief smiles and nods to each other on their way through the front door. Today, no one made motion to do more than shuffle in and stand. Waiting.

But waiting for what?

My mother squeezed my collarbone too tightly, and I squirmed until I tumbled free to skid to a halt before the Tackler. Whereas he normally tucked his lengthy beard beneath his shirt, it rested atop it this morning. His collar was buttoned too tight against slight jowls as he cleared his throat. "Today serves as a warning to us all," he said as he flicked his gaze in my direction. "Everyone plays a role in Dekwood, and when someone doesn't know their place or steps out of it, they're a danger to our way of life. A danger to us all."

A dozen workers over, a woman stifled her sob. The Tackler sought out the source and finding nothing, continued. "Don't let loose the grieving thoughts that plague you, but instead, put your mind toward the task at hand. Christmas approaches."

The voices that recited his words lacked enthusiasm. "Christmas approaches."

The phrase transformed their faces. Where there had rested sorrow and fear, grim determination lit a fire in their eyes as they departed for their workspaces. My mother shrugged as the masses carried her away from me.

"No trouble today," the Tackler barked at me, and I frowned.

I remained silent until I spotted the empty stool in the carding room. "Where's Charlene?"

Matthew's lip welled with blood where he'd bitten it too hard. I repeated the question, this time while staring directly at him, and the carding brush in his hand snapped in half. "Let it go," he muttered.

"Where is she? And why did the Tackler profess such warnings?"

Like yesterday, they were destined to ignore me. I scooted my stool beside a little one stuffing hunks of wool into a basket. "I don't think we've met. My name is Elise. What's yours?"

"Belinda."

"Don't speak, Belinda. The bells will come." At Matthew's sharp warning, the child wrapped her arms about her legs, her eyes wide.

In the back of my mind, the bells jingled as the moon rose, and I dropped my carding brush. "Matthew, the bells did come. Last night—did they not? Tell me, where is your sister?"

He closed his eyes. "The bells shook the air last night, and the Ringers walked among us. I thought they'd come for you —" he said, stopping to look on me with tearful eyes, "—but they'd come for C-Charlene."

This was my fault. I'd encouraged Charlene to talk against

her better judgment, and because of it, she was gone. "I-I'm sorry, I did not mean—"

"Didn't mean what? To talk Charlene into her death? Because of your talk of schools and magics—as if such things were possible in Dekwood—she went home and begged to be sent away. Can you imagine? She asked *our* father to be sent away so she could learn!"

Anger flushed my cheeks. "Matthew, I never intended for your sister to be taken, but asking to learn should not be a crime. Where exactly has she been taken? By whom? What are Ringers?"

"The Ringers ensure the peace and prosperity in this town. They make sure everyone serves their purpose. When they...they—when they take you, you're dead, Elise. Gone."

I did not recall when I stood, much less when I fled that room, but my running ceased when I reached the smallest building near the center of town: a lone house befitting someone who served Magistrate Revoir de Leunt. Its bricks crumbled a little less, were a little less faded than those around it, and instead of a single-floor dwelling, the house was its own two-story abode. The wailing from inside—a harsh, keening of pain that carried on with few gaps for breath—confirmed my suspicions.

The front step creaked beneath my foot when a shadow moved behind the window, and the same slip of a man from our second day in town leaned out the open doorway to wave an empty fist at me. "Go away! Haven't you done enough to this town?"

"I'm sorry?"

When he laughed, the wailing inside grew louder. "You watch it, girl. They'll be coming for you next!"

His words should have scared me, but the fluttering inside my stomach ceased as the earth beneath me hummed. Somewhere out there, someone called on the magics deep within the soil. Someone out there was not as backward thinking as the villagers. Someone out there was educated.

But not Nicolas. For all Charlene's belief that her father owned magical texts, not a single drop of power sang in his blood or whispered in his breath.

To him, I said, "I am quite sure they will seek me out, sir, and when they do, I have questions for them."

"You won't be able to ask."

"Why?" I asked, and the crying inside paused.

"Because when they come, they suck out your soul." He retreated and slammed the door behind him, but not even solid oak could drown out the cries inside.

Death magic. It had to be.

If the Ringers took ownership of people's souls, then for what purpose? Fuel? Something to power the dark magics required for the undead to walk the earth? Who would do such a thing? Who could?

I stared at the shadowed mansion that hovered in the distance. The only person people feared outside the Ringers was the magistrate. He possessed power and money enough to control an entire town. And if the rumors were true, he was ancient and learned—learned enough to make my knowledge of magic a mere thimbleful.

The thought filled me with dread.

No matter what words were uttered, Papa stood firm. "Their ways aren't ours, but we're here now. Keep your head down until we send you to the Academe."

"But Charlene is missing." My mother's chair scraped across the floor as she excused herself, and I asked, "What reason do we have to remain in this town?"

"Just a smidgen longer, Elise."

"Papa—"

He closed his eyes a moment. "We owe the magistrate for putting us up here. To leave would be a mark against us."

"Do we need his favor so much then?"

Papa sighed. "A man like that—he'd keep you from school with only a frown. Don't court trouble. By mid-spring, summer at the latest, we should have the means to leave."

I fled, crossing the hall to my room. He had never been a man of excuses before, any more than my mother had allowed her appearance to falter or her tongue to still. Sleep avoided me as I stared, opened eyed, at the cracks in the ceiling until long after the hum of my parents' conversation changed to snores. When snowflakes tapped against my room's tiny window, I rubbed the sleeve of my nightshirt against the pane to stare out across the town below.

The street should have been bare this late hour, but diminutive twinkles danced in the air, cast off from the shimmer below. Rather than look away, I gaped as five white horses took form beneath my window. Five muzzles snuffed the falling snowflakes. One shook his head and sent up an eerie peal as the bells on his harness jingled—less a jingle and more like the scream of cold air across one's skin.

These weren't mere horses, and the five men astride them weren't mere men.

Red coats clung to gray flesh that stretched too taut over skeletal frames, and the mouth that grinned at me tugged at the corners until it might have split the near-translucent skin. This Ringer—his blue eyes ghostly and glowing—bore a sash across his red jacket, decorated with symbols burned black into the fabric.

Even from the inn's second floor, far from the touch of the earth, the thrum of magic in the air seeped into my feet. The bells rattled my ears as the horses stepped forward.

I flung my heavy jacket over my nightshirt and stuffed my

socked feet in my boots. I threw open the door. Halfway down the stairs, I recalled the hour and slowed my steps to a creep.

The bolt was thrown over the inn's entrance; I shoved it upright with a grunt.

By the time the bitter chill outside blustered my face and threatened to rip the air from my lungs, the Ringers were gone.

Snow filled in the edges of the hoof prints. I followed them down the main street and around the corner toward the edge of town. In the distance, the forest darkened an already dark night, and I closed my eyes before I stepped across the town's threshold.

If they'd crossed into the forest, I'd never find them. Something...or someone whined to my left, and I followed the sound into a partially fenced yard. Tucked back against the trees lay a house made of lean-to boards and half-rotted wooden planks. A sagging roof groaned under the snow's weight and out front stood five white horses. I hurried my steps.

Inside the house, another whine, then a cry, and the air outside warmed. The snow stopped, and my feet sweated inside my leather boots. Magic. *Dangerous* magic.

I didn't know what kind, but the power of it made my vision swim. I stepped sideways to avoid the horse droppings. Horse droppings? Where they real beasts then? One of the horses shoved his muzzle into my shoulder blade, and I flinched.

The horses were living creatures. But what about the Ringers themselves?

My hand paused on the curtain that served as the house's

front door. When a child screamed, I stumbled over my boots as I pushed my way through thick wool. Five beings who had once been men shimmered in the main room. One stood over a child no older than four, who cowered in his mother's arms. Tears stained the child's reddened cheeks and snot gummed up his nose, but no sound or breath escaped his blue lips.

His mother screamed at the Ringer, and when he touched his knotted hand to her flesh, her lips parted round.

I snapped my eyes shut, and inside my boots the soles of my feet burned.

Outside the air split with a cacophony of jingling bells, and when I pried open my eyes, two corpses lay in the corner, their hands tangled in one another's.

They weren't vanished or disappeared as Charlene had implied.

They were dead.

Seven

TWO DAYS UNTIL CHRISTMAS

"What did you do?" Papa's voice carried more than a warning with the question, and I winced.

"There was magic; I could feel it! I needed to see what these Ringers were about," I said. My mother tore apart the roll in her hands, leaving little breadcrumbs scattered across the table's edge. Preoccupied with watching her, I failed to see Papa move until his hands seized mine in too tight a grip as he stood beside my chair.

"Don't follow them again. Leave it alone. Promise me now."

"But—"

"Do as you're told!" he snapped, and I tugged my hands away. "I'm-I'm sorry I snapped, Elise, but this is dangerous. This isn't growing a tree in the backyard or blossoming a flower in a vase. It's dangerous magic—the kind that comes with decades of learning and leads to evil beings and death. A-and I can't lose you." His voice caught, and what was left of my mother's bread fell to her plate with a thud.

"I need more time to clear our debt to the magistrate.

49

Please mind me," he begged, and I nodded. After that, neither of my parents ate.

When my mother and I walked to the factory that morning, we passed the coroner's carriage. A trio of men moved two bodies wrapped in blankets—one child-sized and both bundled with care.

"Is that...?" my mother asked.

"Yes."

She wrapped an arm across my shoulder and squeezed. "Listen to your father, Elise. Please."

Up ahead, Papa spoke to Mr. Ashton. Whatever words Mr. Ashton spoke caused Papa's face to pale.

"We'll be late, Elise."

"I'll catch up," I said to my mother, who placed a hand over her swelling middle as she clambered through the snow without me. Papa furrowed his brows when he spotted me, but I hid in the shadow of the coroner's carriage until Mr. Ashton retreated.

"Why aren't you with your mother?" Papa asked when I finally approached.

"I forgot something. Was that Charlene's father?"

Papa nodded. "We're moving out of the inn in a few days' time. Probably after Christmas. Magistrate Leunt has found us a place."

My stomach sank. "Where?"

"Just at the edge of town. It's in rough shape, little more than a lean-to at the moment, but they're going to repair it for us. Can't have your mother expecting in a place as drafty as that. Now hurry along to work."

If the cold air hadn't made my teeth chatter, the news would have done so. The home that would be ours had belonged to the two victims, and the thought of dwelling in such a place sickened me. Would our taking such a home further indebt us to this magistrate?

Papa watched me until I had turned the corner, but I waited twenty heartbeats—long enough for him to leave—before I returned to the statue at the town's center. There was something about this mysterious magistrate we never glimpsed —this magistrate in charge of a town of fear and death.

Animating the dead wasn't impossible, but it was forbidden for a reason.

I glanced into the statue's face. *Are you behind this?*

The stone eyes blinked.

I tumbled backward to land on my rear in the snow.

"It's how he knows." The voice belonged to a man buried in rags reeking of body odor. He ran a hand through graying, oily hair that hung a few inches past the tips of his ears.

"Who? The magistrate?"

"Who else? The man in control. He watches. He listens. And when you ain't right, the red men come."

"The red men? You mean the Rin—"

The hand he clamped over my mouth soured my stomach; it stank of blood and earth. I wriggled, and he pulled his hands away. "Don' say their name. Gives them power."

"What are they? Are they reanimated corpses or something more?"

He shrugged. "Does it matter? Until Christmas passes, no one is safe."

"I know things, sir. Magics. Basic practice, but I could—"

The man shrank back at the word. The coroner's carriage stopped beside us, and a gentleman in a crisp, black suit approached. "Mr. Henry, come with me. It's time to see to Elizabeth and the boy."

The man's face crumpled at the name, and he allowed himself to be ushered into the carriage and away from the watching eyes of the statue.

The carriage set off in the direction of the mansion. If there were answers to be had, they would be there.

No magician worth his salt worked without a library. No one. It was long past the hour to discover what this magistrate was hiding, though it would have to wait. Another day's work missed would be noticed.

The hours dragged along as I carded wool in silence. Everyone gave me wide berth, and for once I did not mind. Papa spent dinner alternating between peering at me from behind his soup spoon and pausing with his mouth open, though he said nothing at all.

That evening, when I watched behind the frosted glass of my window, the Ringers and their horses materialized directly below me. The shortest one, with green eyes of a color that could melt hearts, peered at me beneath his red cap. When he hooked a finger and beckoned to me, I threw the shutters closed with a snap and fell beneath my covers until the jingling bells faded, and the sun crept over the horizon.

Christmas Eve had begun.

Eight

CHRISTMAS EVE

I abandoned the inn before the town awoke and sought the lone path to the mansion. While I thought myself alone, red weaved itself against the drift covered trees and cobble. In the light of my oil lantern, I thought the trees painted with blood until the red moved. A person perhaps?

The figure ahead turned his green eyes on me.

He was alone, Ringer though he was, and when he beckoned for me to follow, my boots crunched in the fresh snow as we approached the mansion.

A grand porch of white stone led to wooden doors bearing stained glass depictions of angelic figures. Circular turrets framed the house on either side, topped by clay-tile spires and iron finials. When the Ringer's boot heel touched the first of twelve steps, the stone didn't shift, nor did the snow depress under his weight.

"Wait!" I whispered, but he gestured at the darkened porch. "I know, you want me to follow, but...are you real?"

His deep green irises marked his sorrow, and he inclined his head once I reached out a trembling hand to touch his coat's fabric, but he leaned away from my grasp. His breath came in little puffs as he pointed again to the front door.

He did not progress beyond the first step, though his muscles strained and tugged as if he wished nothing more than to proceed. A small eight-pointed star was burned into the left side of the door frame, and when I touched it, it burned my thumb through my gloves.

"You can't pass…because whatever ties you to this world is here? In this mansion?"

His direct look intensified the burn that coursed through my thumb. "S-s " He grimaced as his tongue hung from the side of his mouth. "S-s-sa-save."

"Save? Or safe?"

"S-save us. All." The bells called out in the distance, and he clenched his hands at his side. "Save."

His figure wavered before it disappeared, and the snow fell in earnest. The doorknob turned beneath my hand, and the door swung open to an entryway of shadows and silence.

Was I expected? Or had the Ringer opened the door?

I muffled a cough in my sleeve as my dry mouth choked on the dust floating through the air. The steps of a grand staircase were draped in rugs long since faded and crushed. When nothing beyond the dust moved, I released my breath in little puffs that danced before me in the chill.

Melting snow left droplets along the wooden floor as I approached the first door on my right. A seating area, followed by a dining room with a table long enough to fit our family, cousins included. Beyond that lay the kitchens and pantry, a smaller eating area, a second living area, and a music room. My fingers lingered on the grand piano, leaving dust trails across the black and yellowed keys.

My breathing quickened, and the wind creaked through invisible gaps in the walls as I approached the grand staircase. The old rugs muffled most of my footfalls as I ascended to the second floor, and once there, I paused outside a room whose open door left a sliver of light in the hallway.

I nudged the door an inch, and when no one shouted or leapt at me, I opened it to a room clear of dust and loneliness.

The library.

Shelf-lined walls held books with gilded covers and lettering in more languages than I had ever seen. In the center of the room, a single desk rested, its velvet-lined top devoid of stationery or ink. The first bookshelf held histories of one kind or another, and I had almost skipped it when I spotted the eight-pointed star near the top: a heavy volume whose cracked spine read *The Accountes & Affairs of the Famile Revoir du Leunt.*

Once I had coaxed the book from its shelf, I settled into the corner with an unobstructed view of the doorway. Not that there was anywhere to hide, but it might have been possible to tuck myself underneath the desk. I squinted at the cramped handwriting on the first dozen pages. Mostly accounts of births and property acquisition, I skimmed first paragraphs until I spotted the pattern of dots in the top right corner of each page.

16: 05, 06, 07...the counting of years or months? The code was familiar to me from my studies. The halfway point of the book held the date of 1693, so supposing the dots' arrangement meant years I flipped to the last page, which was blank.

Was the magistrate adding to this book? I backtracked until I reached pages bearing a style of loose-flowing handwriting that was lengthy in stroke. The last entry was dated almost a century ago in the year of 1743. Blotch marks sprinkled their way across the yellowed page, and the handwriting shifted as his emotions overwhelmed him:

My boys—all dead—Nothing good and pure and wholesome comes from a woman, this one more than most as her wyld and evyl ways brought my young Eli to ruin. There is naught more foolish than a young boy in love, and doubly so when in love with a sorceress.

She thrice scoffed him before the town and his brothers rose to his aide, as brothers should. For nigh two hours they battled this sorceress and sought to drive off her evyl spells from this village, but ne'er had they fought with such a foul creature.

I came upon their bare bodies in the centre of town, my sons' corpses drained of life and warped by magics far darker than taught by decent sorcerers. And she stood above them, her smile as grim as the winter's new sun. I will remember her words until my death.

"Your sons thought to best me, Magistrate Revoir du Leunt. I merely wished to walk alone, but Eli would have none of it. Obsessed he was. An unhealthy and unholy sickness was upon him."

Sorceress she may be, but my family's history she knew not, and I smote her where she stood. The ground reached up and buried her in its gaping jaws, but still my sons were dead. Still their bodies lay tossed like stones across the river top.

Tonight, they will wander the land of the dead no more. Tonight, the earth will return to me what was lost, and this town will harbor sorceresses no longer.

The writing ceased, the following pages blank. Not that it mattered. An event over a century ago involving our magistrate—the same magistrate, if the names were to be believed, had cast his sons into the realm of living dead. The skill required to create such beings...

I slid the book back into place. Three more bookcases held a variety of stories and treatises but nothing continuing the family story. Certainly nothing magical. On the last bookcase, I spied a collection of magical texts. Rather than focus on their concealed titles, I shut my eyes and whispered my fingers across their spines. Power ebbed and flowed from them, but my fingertips did not tingle until my hand rested on a slim book wedged between a behemoth of a text and the edge of shelf.

There was more than power to this book. There was hatred and envy and sorrow.

A well-worn yet simple cover—nothing to call attention in a grand library such as this—yet when its pages fell open at my touch, spells of death and life were sketched in grand detail. I shoved the book into my pocket, though it was not far enough away from my heart for comfort.

My lantern flickered as its oil burned low, and I crept away and down the stairs. As I tiptoed with aching, cold feet, I spotted a lengthy picture on the wall whose frame hovered an inch or two above the carpeted floor. An ugly beast all claws and teeth gnashed his way toward the edge of the canvas. In the opposite corner, a woman cloaked in red velvet crouched, her hands glowing as she fought the beast. I removed one hand from a glove and touched the painting.

Nothing. No response.

But it had to be here! Wherever his workroom lay, it would be on the ground floor. Somewhere that would touch the soil of the earth and open to the air and water of the sky. I set my lantern on the floor and, gripping the painting by its frame, tilted it. Behind the painting, the wall was missing.

The weight of the painting near tipped me on my side, yet I heaved it from the wall above to expose the open archway. As I leaned it against the wall, I prayed no one would awaken to notice the painting's misplacement. I brought my lantern into a narrow stairwell that smelled heavily of iron. A dozen steps down brought me to a metal door, which was unlocked.

The bottom corner dragged across the floor with a cry, and I winced as I wrenched it open. Nothing moved above or below, and I stepped across the threshold into an almost empty room: four bare walls, one archway walled off, and one wobbly-looking chair in the corner. The lone window near the ceiling confirmed I was in a basement. The perfect sorcerer's workroom.

Yet no sigils decorated the sparse room—not even the eight-pointed star that had burned my thumb.

A shift in weight caused the stairs outside to groan. Someone stood outside. I dragged the chair to the window. Even on my tiptoes, I struggled to push the window up and open as its jambs stuck. Outside, bells jingled and a set of hooves stopped before the window.

The Ringer with the green eyes touched the glass, which dissolved with a gust of snow and wind. I pulled my upper half through the window frame and received a face full of snow. More of the powder wiggled its way into my coat as I shimmied through. My jacket caught on the latch, and I gave it a firm tug before tumbling outside.

Something old and angry mumbled inside the room I'd vacated, and the ground beneath me trembled. With no care for the tracks left behind, I tossed up snow as I bolted toward town. Halfway to the inn, the bells ceased, and the earth shook no more.

My breath struggled in my chest until I crawled into my bed, and even then, my thumb throbbed with warmth.

Nine

I slumbered long past the rising sun and woke to shoulder shakes. When I opened my eyes, the shaking relented, though my mother sat on the mattress's edge as worry lines traversed her forehead. "What time is it?" I asked.

"Long past when young ladies should still be lying about. It's near noon."

Her words brought me upright in bed, and I cast aside my blankets in a rush. I crawled over the footboard and around my mother. "Why aren't you at work?" I asked as I dug through the bedside chest.

"I was. I came to check on you. You aren't ill again, are you?" She pressed a cool hand against my forehead, which I shrugged aside in order to pull on a pair of stiff pants. My mother scowled but said nothing about my choice of attire. Tufts of wool clung to her shawl, which she pulled closer about slumped shoulders. I glanced one-too-many times at my bed, and my mother crouched with a groan. Her round belly brushed against the mattress as she tucked her hand between it and the wooden frame. She would have liked to have been up to her shoulder in her search, but my soon-to-be brother didn't allow for it. Either way, she rooted around quite unladylike and undignified.

The woman who'd always taken such care with her appearance resembled the rest of the town—shoddy, rumpled, and tired. Her pointed shoes were faded and scuffed, wisps of pale-blonde hair had escaped her bun, and the bottom of her gray skirt was torn. Whatever nonsense the magistrate used to hold this town in disarray had to be stopped.

My mother's hand came back empty, but I held my breath rather than allow the sigh to escape. She reached for my arm to pull herself upright. I frowned, and she waved her hand in the air. "I thought—never mind. I need to get back to the factory."

Her heavy steps lumbered down each stair step and once she had arrived at the bottom, I retrieved the book I'd "borrowed" from the very back corner of the mattress. Simple bound, black leather with only the title etched in silver lettering: *Mort de Vie*.

Cold as it would be outside, I could not be caught reading this. My boots went on first, followed by my heavy wool coat, then a cream-colored scarf that reeked of mothballs, and matching woolen gloves. Lastly, I tucked the small book into my coat pocket and set out for somewhere quiet.

Despite the pallor over Dekwood, the sun glinted off the snow, nearly blinding me as I headed for the edge of town. No one would think to seek me out at the house that eventually would be ours, especially not with repairs set to begin after Christmas.

The heavy curtain was missing from the doorframe, making me glad for my coat's warmth. I avoided the living area where the mother and child had been killed. The sun trickling through a wedge of window cast shadows where they'd lain, and I hurried my steps into the next room. The stove held no warmth, but I drew my own as I noticed a child's letters scribbled across scattered paper on the table. My smile faltered when I studied the page.

The little boy had sketched images of the Ringers.

I leaned on the chair, and when it didn't break, I took my seat and retrieved the book. Its innards lacked the printed text of most books on magic. This one held an older, shakier handwriting. Assuming *The Accountes & Affairs of the Famile Revoir du Leunt* had been penned by the magistrate and his predecessors, this work was by someone—or *something*—else entirely.

Most of the pages held spells—not just incantations or minor cantrips to light a candle or put a hound to sleep—but spells with real power: the kind I'd never see in school, the kind I wouldn't discover until long after I'd grown gray and crooked after the magic corrupted me.

One spell cast the soul of another into that of a beast, while another claimed to keep all ills at bay. When I turned the page, I dropped the book on the table where its spine splintered. *Clochen Mort de Noël.*

Death bells.

It was more than the cold that chilled me as I read. The half I comprehended was enough.

Upon the evenfall of Solstice, submit five upon the land. In the holy circle of Elshirei, draw forth the innocent and pierce the air with peals of five:

> *Thy will it be,*
> *five blind will see.*
> *A year unmade,*
> *until the spade,*
> *doth break this circle*
> *of Christmas that's made,*
> *And set the risen free.*

The circle was easy. Every spell tied into the earth, into the land, but to create a circle of blood to honor Elshirei the Betrayed was an unclean deed. To raise the dead—

A hand touched my shoulder, and I screamed.

"Please, I didn't mean to frighten you." Mr. Henry hovered beside me. The rags he wore stank of booze, but he turned alert eyes on me in that moment. "I knew I felt something—"

He pressed a finger to my thumb, and the burning pulsed. "You've been to the house," he said.

I nodded. "How—"

Mr. Henry rolled down the collar of his scarf to display the *viziol* branded into the bluish skin on his neck. The protruding *V*, which rose from the top of two nested triangles left me slack with relief, and he shook his head. "I know that look. You think I'm here to save you, save this town, but I'm not."

"But you are a sorcerer, trained in the arts of high magic and served with protecting..."

Tears welled up as he cast a glance over his shoulder. "I've done my duty to this world and look where it got me. Elizabeth and Peter dead—their souls used to keep that filth alive for another year. When tomorrow passes, I'll be one more among the many and gladly so."

"Please," I said as he turned to pass, "Tell me what this is. I don't understand this spell or how to stop it."

He laughed a rich, belly laugh. "If I can't stop it, what makes you think a mere whip of a girl like you can? You've not even earned entrance to an Academe, much less gained an apprenticeship."

"I-I...may not be able to cease this spell's grip, but I must try, Mr. Henry. Please tell me what this spell means." I pointed at the paragraph in the book and the drawing beside it of the reanimated corpse with dull eyes and bells tied at its belt loops.

"I can't work the magic anymore, not for a long while. Something the magistrate's doing, I suppose."

"Were you sent here to stop him?"

He shook his head. "Not me, but my grandpa. He gave his life failing, as did my pa. That madman stripped the magic out of folks after that, but there's something...something deep down. A rumbling perhaps. I can feel it in the earth." His breath smelled of rot, and I took short breaths through my mouth. "He's losing control of his boys."

Outside, the wind gusted, and the planks rattled around us. Mr. Henry didn't notice the goosebumps that decorated his bare arms.

"His boys?" I asked.

"Them horsemen—the bell ringers. Those are his sons he's brought back."

"The story then, it is true? About the sorceress killing his sons?"

Mr. Henry nodded. "Rumors are that his sons deserved it. Either way, that spell's how he did it. At first, the mighty Magistrate Leunt did the killing. He slaughtered four women in their sleep that morning—all of them sorceresses —and used the blood to draw his circle. Did it at the Solstice's dawn, the day after his boys died. He anointed silver bells—it must be pure silver mind you—with the same blood and spoke the words. It near killed him from what I've heard, but then, he'd already had spells in place to protect against that."

"How...how old is he? The magistrate?"

"Older than this town. Or maybe not old enough. It doesn't matter." I closed the book, and Mr. Henry nodded. "Good, get your folks out of this town and away from this madness."

I slipped the book in my coat pocket. "I am not leaving. I am going to break the spell." His laughter drove icy air into my resolve, but I stood straight. "A Ringer asked me to try, so I must."

"Now I know you're nothing but silly. The Ringers can't speak."

"But he did—the one with the green eyes—he asked me to save them."

Mr. Henry tilted his head. "Huh. Maybe the magistrate is ready after all. Too many centuries passed him by in his sorrow. Look, if you're determined to do this, it must be tomorrow."

"On Christmas?"

"On the Christmas."

"Why?" I asked.

"The Ringers feed to replenish the circle's seal between Solstice, when they rise, and Christmas, when they sleep. Look again at the spell."

I retrieved the book and turned to the proper page. Mr. Henry pointed to tiny scribblings near the edge of the page. "The blood cord protect for five full days," I read, then shook my head. "I don't understand."

"To renew the seal, he must remove his protections."

"...And the circle will be vulnerable!"

He nodded. "But you still have to get to it. He'll see you coming. He has his eye on you yet, I'd wager."

"I'm counting on it."

"MOTHER?"

She laid aside her knitting and waited. How she found the energy after a long day working the factory loom was beyond my comprehension, but every evening since we had arrived, she prepared for my brother's birth. "Hmmm?"

"I need you and Papa to do me a favor." Papa, who'd been

stretched out across the bed, sat up, eyes open, and I swallowed hard. "In the morning, I need you to gather the folks in town at the statue. Get everyone to bring all the bells they can —silver bells—"

"Is this about those funny fellas in the red coats? Didn't I tell you to stay away from that evilness?"

My toes curled in my stockings at Papa's questions. "How'd you know about their red coats?"

"Saw them just last night."

"If you see them again, flee. They are killers."

"That's what Frederick at work said. I know I told you to keep your head down, but something wasn't right with how they looked. I couldn't get warm after seeing them." He stared at his knees.

"They are the magistrate's sons, Papa. They died over a hundred years ago, but he brought them back from beyond. He uses the town to keep them alive." The entire story poured forth and by the time I'd finished, my mother was tossing her belongings into a chest. "What are you doing?" I asked.

"Packing. We're not staying here," she muttered.

"That's not a bad idea. Papa, you two should leave. At least until Christmas passes."

"And what makes you think you aren't coming with us? Debt be damned," he said.

I left their room and crossed into mine where I retrieved the book from its hiding place. When I returned, I closed their door behind me and set it on the table.

"What is that?" Papa asked.

"It is a book on dark magics. Foul spells that call for the murder of innocent people. I found it in the magistrate's house."

My mother hissed, "You trespassed?"

"I had to know what purpose he served in—"

"And now that you do, you'll what? Use that book against

him? If he's really as old as you say, you won't touch him with the little tricks you know. Besides, no daughter of mine will commit such...ungodly acts!" Papa had found his feet halfway through the tumble of words, and the door slammed as he left.

My mother's knitting needles remained untouched on the table beside the book. "What will you do...if I gather the townspeople?"

"The Ringers will seek out the statue—imagine, a town full of unwillful people— and when I hear the bells, I will know he is vulnerable. I will break the circle with a single smudge. The spell will be broken."

"Surely it can't be that easy."

"Magic is organic. It comes from the earth and the air, the beings around us, and our will. If you remove any of those components, magic dissipates and returns to its natural state. The circle can't be protected if he means to renew it."

I withheld the mention that I'd be trespassing...again, not to mention the danger of crossing a magical circle, vulnerable or not.

She shook her head, and a gray curl fell across her cheekbone. "I'm not sure I understand it, but if you say you can do this, I believe you. Everyone will be at the statue on Christmas if I have to drag them there at needlepoint."

I snatched the book from the table and turned away so she wouldn't see the tears in my eyes.

Ten

CHRISTMAS DAY

The crisp morning of Christmas dawned across Dekwood— the one day of the year no one worked. Families would gather to eat and celebrate the coming of a new year, of new opportunities, and new beginnings. Sometime after sunrise, Papa would wake as usual and give thanks to *Wothan* for the sacrifices made in our honor. The town, assuming they followed tradition, would sacrifice five cattle—cows if they had it, though sheep would also honor the All-Father. While children dreamed of the gift giving to come, I crept from my bed and into the pre-dawn's falling snow.

Five horses stood in the field nearby, their bells removed as they pawed through the snow for whatever grasses lay underneath. The magistrate's mansion felt hollow to the touch, but where else would a mourning father be but here with his sons?

He would expect me through the front door—that plan would fail. I backed down the steps until my boots touched soil, then I slid first one foot and then the other from my boots. My stockings came next until I shivered barefooted in the snow.

While my feet froze, my skin hummed with the power beneath me. Around the mansion's side, the basement's window waited as paneless as I had left it. The room stood empty, but the chair had been returned to the corner. I drew a circle in the snow with an ungloved finger and picked up a pinch, which melted in my hands. The water droplets returned to the snow as I whispered.

Inside the room, the chair wobbled.

Sweat broke out across my brow, and I removed my wool hat, which I stuffed into my coat pocket. Nothing could leave the circle, not even to join the pile my boots and stockings made nearby. I dug my fingernails into my palms and focused.

Move the chair. Move the chair.

Still the chair merely wobbled.

The barest hints of sun peeked over the horizon, and I closed my eyes to the distraction. The chair trembled. A light scratching as it then slid an inch and another. I panted as drips of sweat sprinkled to land inside my circle. A thud of wood against stone rang out, and I opened my eyes.

Without breaking the circle, I leaned forward and peered down. The chair rested against the wall a few inches to the left of the window. The power drained from me in a rush, and I broke the circle with my chilled finger.

Despite the ache in my toes, my boots remained outside as I slid feet first through the window. I landed too hard on the chair, which fell over and toppled me on my side. Inside the empty room, I sighed and rubbed my hip where I had landed.

Nothing led to the location of his circle. The floor was cold stone, smooth and polished and completely unyielding to my probe for a power source.

I took out the silver ring in my pocket. It had been a gift from my parents, the single piece of silver to serve as the root. If I wished to study at the Academe, this ring was required to cast the compulsory entry spell. An expensive cost for our family but worth the price.

If I used it now, I might never set foot in the Academe.

Two bodies haunted me, and I whispered. The power inside the ring hummed and warmed my fingers. I allowed the warmth to wash over me, and when I brushed my fingers along the wall, a bell on the other side cried out in pain.

"Open," I whispered, and the silver ring dissolved into vapor. The air around me sizzled, and the stone wall wavered five heartbeats before disappearing to reveal a workroom. The walls remained of gray-slab stone, but the floor was compacted dirt and lacked the typical smells of manure and greenery. I poked a single finger in it and listened.

The soil was dead.

A rut formed the circle, its insides rimmed with fresh blood. At its center lay a single bell. Simple and plain, with no ornamentation and a single dent. The bell's original bloody baptism had long faded. I couldn't cross the circle, not yet. Not if I wished to remain living.

Again a squeak on the steps alerted me to a guest, and I leaned against the wall and breathed while my muscles screamed to flee. My feet burned as someone halted outside the visible doorway.

"It's been far too long since there's been a touch on the soil other than my own."

The voice was rich and deep and reminded me of my late grandfather. Far too kind a voice for someone exercising such atrocities. The man who stepped inside lacked the wrinkles his retreating hairline professed he should have. When he glanced at me, his eyes lacked his voice's humor. They carried the empty framing of winter, cold and dead.

I stepped away from him, careful not to touch the circle. The magistrate followed me, and I edged as close to the circle as I could. When he touched the top of my head, my vision swam. "So like her you are," he whispered. "And like her, you've stolen away Eli."

"Eli?"

"My son. He should ride the town with his brothers, yet he hovers behind to watch you. He always carried a heart sickness within him. Horsewhipped by the mere sight of a woman."

I melted under the layers of clothing: rugged pants tucked into men's boots; a plain, button-up shirt; and a coat hanging past my knees. No curves, nothing pink, and certainly nothing womanly about me. "I'm more likely to be mistaken for a boy than a woman. I've not distracted your son, sir. He wishes to die."

"He's already dead."

"Not completely. The bell ties him to this world. He wishes to rest."

The magistrate stepped across the circle. "Simpering fool was always the weak one. Maybe it's time to replace him." He reached for the bell.

"Wait!" I shouted, and his gnarled hand stopped mid-reach. "Why do you keep them animated like this? To serve what purpose?"

"To serve life! My sons were unfairly and untimely ripped from me at the prime of their youth. Why ask such questions though, when you already know this having been in my library."

His thumb smudged a blood droplet as he retrieved the bell. It sounded once, and Eli materialized before us. I scooted closer to the door until my back leaned against a workbench. Now that he was within the circle, I could not break it.

Eli's green eyes glowed in the room's dimness. "Kill me," he whispered, and the magistrate clenched his fist around the bell.

"After all I've done for you and your brothers, you truly beg for death?"

I glanced over my shoulder. A lantern flickered on the table.

While Magistrate Leunt argued with his son, I reached back and grasped the lantern by its base. Its heat burned my fingers for a moment before I tossed it across the circle's threshold. Its glass casing shattered, and the spilled oil caught in a bright flash of flame.

"Dammit," the magistrate muttered and shoved the bell into his pants' pocket. He removed his jacket and used it to beat the flames. Eli swiveled and nodded once in my direction. My thoughts were correct.

Arrogant as the day, the magistrate had failed to protect against non-human physical intrusions.

While he danced with the flames, I smeared my bare foot across the dirt and broke the physical circle. The shock drove the magistrate to his knees as the circle howled, and I retrieved the bell from his pocket.

I had but a minute before he would recover, so I made the only choice available to someone as thoroughly outclassed as I was—I ran.

Boots abandoned, I pounded up the stairs in quite the unladylike fashion. The bell in my hands rang louder than my footfalls, and I burst through the front door as I struggled to listen over the sounds of my haggard breath. Halfway to the statue, I heard them.

Bells.

Hundreds of bells rattling and clanging and jingling as the sun blessed the Christmas day. Behind me, hoof beats on the road approached.

Mr. Henry had clambered up to the statue's arms, where he beckoned for me to hurry.

Between gasps, I shouted at him, "The horse's bells...are ringing! Why...Why haven't they...stopped?"

"We need a circle!" called Mr. Henry.

My feet were nearly numb, but the snow's sting sharpened my focus. There was no time to draw a circle this large. "Quick, make a circle! Shoulder to shoulder, and ring the bells!" I shouted.

Some villagers stopped ringing their bells when they spotted me; none of them made an effort to form a circle beyond my parents, and even they cocked their heads at the request.

The Ringers stopped before the group, and several villagers dropped their bells. A child cried—a whimpering hiccup that awoke the town to the danger before them. Several stepped back while others made motion to leave.

Mr. Henry stopped their flight by clapping his hands together. "Here's your chance. You can fall prey to the Ringers, or you can do what she says. Make a circle and keep ringing those bells! For Elizabeth and Peter and Charlene and countless others we've lost to the bells."

Like a well-manned loom, they circled around the statue with each person's shoulder pressed up against the next as they rang the bells of Christmas. I stood in the middle and called out to Mr. Henry. "Now what?"

"Destroy the bell."

"What? How? The power—"

"Is broken. It's just a bell."

One Ringer reached for the woman in front of him. I held the bell in both hands and snapped its wooden handle. Both pieces tumbled to the ground. Blood coursed off the silver to pool in the snow. The Ringers shrieked—ungodly sounds of torture and joy—yet one set of green eyes found mine. Tears pooled in Eli's eyes as he smiled.

A few villagers paused in their ringing, and Mr. Henry cried out, "Keep ringing those bells."

I fished the bell out from the bloody pool and wiped off the remaining droplets with the corner of my jacket. Once clean, I held the bell by its crown and gave it five chimes.

Five brothers faded from the world. Five sets of bells fell tarnished to the snow below.

And in the distance, a disheveled man rode toward us. I pushed my way through the villagers until I stood as a shield before them.

They filed in behind me, a united wall as the magistrate approached. His years weighed on him like sand; his skin sagged as he dismounted. Each step grayed his hair until it flashed white, and his shoulders curled in on his frame until he hunched over—one lone man before the people of Dekwood.

"Magistrate?" a woman whispered, and he cupped a hand to his ear.

"Say again?"

"Do you know where you are, Magistrate?"

He frowned at her. "No, where am I?" His eyes blinked. When he met my gaze, recognition lit them. He raised a finger in my direction, but Mr. Henry placed himself before me. The *viziol* on his neck pulsed.

"Your magic has returned?" I asked.

He nodded, and the magistrate flinched. Mr. Henry touched his thumb to the old man's forehead. Five counts before the magistrate cackled and tumbled away. His feet carried him to his horse. The effort would cost him, but he mounted swiftly with another cackle. His horse's bells released a sour note as he galloped for the forest of the dead.

"Should we pursue him?" I asked, and Mr. Henry shrugged.

"The spells he used have warped him. Hard to say whether he has any real magic left."

"Good riddance," someone cried, and others muttered similar statements.

My mother draped an arm around my shoulder and pressed her lips to my head. I shivered in the Christmas sun. "Can somebody fetch me some shoes? I seem to have left mine behind."

Laughter draped the village in a glow, and behind me, someone said, "Dearie, you can have whatever you want."

Spring brought life to the village. My mother gave birth to my brother, Saul, and the village of Dekwood established Mr. Henry as the town sorcerer. They bestowed the magistrate's mansion on him, though he never set foot inside. Rather than linger with the illness such dark magics cast upon a place, he rebuilt his home at the edge of town and set about restoring the success of its people.

The magistrate never returned to Dekwood.

Some believed he could be heard cackling madly in the forest of the dead, which never grew again, while others said he blew away in the wind that swept over the village in the coming days. Others still told tales of his voice ringing out in the highest pitches of the jingling bells deep in winter.

The bells returned no one, but their jingle held a bitter sweetness for the people of Dekwood until such a time as they forgot the Ringers. When the villagers kept their fear no longer, the forest returned and the looms sang songs of the people's bravery. They smiled to think of the magic that had saved them.

And the red-headed girl behind the magic.

Afterword

I can't take all the credit for this story as the baseline idea for it came from my husband. We were driving around Seattle when he said, "What if jingle bells were the bringers of evil? The sound summoned something from our nightmares?" His questions spun other questions in me. All of our fairytales and mythos have fragments of truth to them. What if Christmas bells did as well?

My brain envisioned undead creatures in red riding white horses through the snow as they traveled to a Victorian town straight out of a Dickens' novel. Once there, they would feed on the souls of the outspoken and the misbehaved. The town knew they were coming by the jingling of bells. Just think of how well the lyrics to *Santa Claus is Coming to Town* fit with this picture? And thus, the Ringers were born.

Raven Oak

Acknowledgments

I would like to thank the many people whose hands touched this story in some way, including my editor, Mimi the "Grammar Chick;" alpha readers Maia Chance, Janine Southard, and Gayle Clemans; and other folks who read early drafts during stressful times.

I also have many thanks to send to the *Ladies of the Write* (especially Kat Richardson) for their copious and detailed suggestions; to Editor Claire Eddy & the Cascade Writers for their copious feedback. I also send copious thanks to my readers, friends, family, and last but not least, my partner, Erk.

About the Author

Photo by St. Photography Studios

Multi-international award-winning speculative fiction author Raven Oak is best known for **Amaskan's Blood** (2016 Ozma Fantasy Award Winner, Epic Awards Finalist, & Reader's Choice Award Winner), **Amaskan's War** (2018 UK Wishing Award YA Finalist), and **Class-M Exile**. She also has many published over a dozen short stories in anthologies and magazines. She's even published on the moon! (No, really!) Raven spent most of her K-12 education doodling stories and 500 page monstrosities that are forever locked away in a filing cabinet.

Besides being a writer and artist, she's a geeky, disabled ENBY who enjoys getting her game on with tabletop games, indulging in cartography and art, or staring at the ocean. She lives in the Seattle area with her partner, and their three kitties who enjoy lounging across the keyboard when writing deadlines approach. Her hair color changes as often as her bio does, and you can find her at **www.ravenoak.net**.

You can *Join the Conspiracy,* her official mailing list to gain information and freebies at http://www.ravenoak.net/for-read ers/mailing-list/ Besides her website, Raven Oak can be found online at the following:

facebook.com/authorroak

twitter.com/raven_oak

instagram.com/author_raven_oak

youtube.com/kaonevar

goodreads.com/raven_oak

bookbub.com/authors/raven-oak

amazon.com/Raven-Oak/e/B00P5PT4AM

Also by Raven Oak

<u>The Boahim Universe</u>

Amaskan's Blood

Amaskan's War

*Amaskan's Honor**

*Ear to Ear**

<u>The Xersian Struggle Universe</u>

*The Eldest Silence**

Class-M Exile

<u>Stand-Alone Works</u>

Ol' St. Nick

The Ringers

From the Worlds of Raven Oak: A Coloring Book

Hungry

The Loss of Luna

Peace Be With You Friend

Dragon Springs & Other Things: A Short Story Collection Book I

Space Ships & Other Trips: A Short Story Collection Book II

*Inocen Lost**

* Forthcoming

Like What You've Read?

Word of mouth is the number one **best** way to ensure that your favorite authors have continued success—better than any paid advertisement.

If you enjoyed this book, please consider leaving a **review** or starred ranking on Amazon, Barnes & Noble, Goodreads, and other retail or reviewer sites.

Your review is greatly appreciated.

www.ingramcontent.com/pod-product-compliance
Lightning Source LLC
Chambersburg PA
CBHW070517200726
48293CB00007B/2586